DAMIAN DROOTH SUPERSLEUTH

Gruesome Ghosts

by Barbara Mitchelhill

illustrated by Tony Ross

STONE ARCH BOOKS
a capstone imprint

First published in the United States in 2011
by Stone Arch Books
A Capstone Imprint
151 Good Counsel Drive, P.O. Box 669
Mankato, Minnesota 56002
www.capstonepub.com

First published in 2009
by Andersen Press Ltd, London

*Library of Congress Cataloging-in-Publication Data is available on the
Library of Congress website.*

Library binding: 978-1-4342-1639-7

Graphic Designer: Kay Fraser
Production Specialist: Michelle Biedscheid

Table of Contents

Chapter 1

Even though I'm famous for my detective work, until last week, I had never had to solve a ghost crime.

Kidnappings, yes. Robberies, yes. But ghosts? No.

But then, last week, when I took on the Case of the Gruesome Ghosts. It turned out to be the most spooky and dangerous case EVER.

It started like this.

We had a new girl at our school. Her name was Annabelle Harrington-Smythe. She was a year older than me, and she had great big blue eyes and long blond hair. I wrote down these facts in my detective's notebook and did a drawing for my records.

Last Wednesday, I was waiting at the playground when I noticed her sitting on a bench with Dixie Stanton (who is really annoying). I was close enough that I could hear what they were saying.

"It's terrible," said Annabelle. "My grandparents have ghosts in their house."

"Cool!" said Dixie Stanton.

"No. Not cool," said Annabelle, biting her lower lip. "There are noises and everything. I can't stay there anymore. It's too scary."

It was clear to me that she was worried, so I stepped forward. "You sound like you need my help," I said.

She looked up at me and frowned. I was a little annoyed when she said, "What can you do? You're just a kid."

Obviously, since she was new to the area, she hadn't heard of my reputation as a detective.

"I may be a kid," I replied, "but I have a super-speed brain."

All she said was "Really?"

Then she walked off with Dixie Stanton,
giggling. That's girls for you.

I didn't let it bother me, though. I
was going to show her how smart I was.
How? By solving her grandparents' ghost
problem. This is how I did it.

First, I called a meeting of my trainee
detectives. They are mostly in my grade
(except Lavender, who is only six). I told
them my plan.

"Before we can do anything," I explained, "I have to get the facts. So I'll go see Annabelle's grandparents and discuss the problem."

Todd said, "Why would they talk to you, Damian? You're not a grown-up."

"Simple," I said. "I'll dress up as a reporter. I'll say I'm doing an article for the paper. They'll talk to me then."

Winston stood with his arms folded and shook his head. "You're a little small for a reporter," he said.

"I can make myself taller," I replied.

"Impossible," said Todd.

I was beginning to get annoyed. "I can make myself taller with Mom's high-heeled boots. But I'll need a pair of long jeans to cover them."

Harry Houseman, the tallest boy in our grade, was the obvious choice.

"How about lending me yours, Harry?" I asked.

He stood looking at me, thinking (which takes Harry quite a long time). Eventually he said, "You can borrow my jeans if I can be on the ghost case with you. I've never seen a ghost."

I wasn't sure. I usually work alone on difficult cases.

But Harry really wanted to be part of the investigation. "If you let me," he said, "you can have my dad's black coat too. That'll make you look like a real reporter."

How could I refuse? With high-heeled boots, long jeans, and a black coat, it was a perfect disguise. The only other thing that I needed was a false mustache.

Luckily, I had already made one from some pieces of brown yarn I found in Mom's room.

"Okay, Harry," I said. "It's a deal. You can come on the case."

He was really excited. "I'll bring my camera," he said. "I can be the photographer."

It wasn't a bad idea. Harry looked like an adult. After all, he was as tall as Mr. Grimethorpe, our teacher.

We planned to visit Annabelle's grandparents the next day, after school. Once I'd solved this case, Annabelle would take me seriously and treat me with respect.

Chapter 2

On Thursday morning, I stuffed my disguise into my gym bag and told Mom I'd be late getting home from school.

"Football practice," I said. (I don't like telling lies, but sometimes, because of my job, I have to.)

After school, Harry and I got ready to walk to Annabelle's grandparents' house. It wasn't far away, but it took forever because of Mom's high-heeled boots.

Walking was IMPOSSIBLE. My toes were scrunched up into the pointy toes and I wobbled so much that I fell over twice. I had to hang on to Harry.

Annabelle's grandparents lived in a huge house on Rigby Road. It had a big yard and big iron gates in front.

"They must be really rich," said Harry. I pushed the gates open and we made our way to the front door and knocked.

After we waited forever, an old lady came and opened it. I knew it must be Annabelle's grandma. She was very old and wrinkly and wearing pink fluffy slippers.

"Yes?" she said, staring right at us. She squinted at us because of her bad eyesight.

"I'm a reporter from the *Evening Post*," I said. (This was another lie I had to make.) "Could I ask you a few questions?"

She looked puzzled. Harry waved his camera in the air and grinned at her. "I'm the photographer," he said, which seemed to make her even more confused.

"I think you'd better come in," she said. "My husband will talk to you."

Dr. Harrington-Smythe (Annabelle's grandpa) was sitting in a chair by the fire, reading the paper.

"These young men are reporters, dear," his wife said.

The doctor folded his paper, looked up and stared. "Reporters? Well, well, well. I know that policemen look younger these days — but now reporters are looking like schoolboys." He threw his head back and laughed. I noticed that he had a set of perfect teeth like Annabelle. But were they real?

"I'm here to write an article," I said, pulling out my notebook and waving my pencil. "About the ghosts."

When she heard the word "ghosts,"
Mrs. Harrington-Smythe gasped and
began to tremble. She was obviously
SCARED STIFF.

The doctor frowned and leaned
forward. "I'm afraid my wife is very
nervous," he said. "It's all because of the
noises in the night. You may think this is
ridiculous, but we've seen things, too."

"Seen things? Like ghosts?" I asked. This was getting interesting. I was writing tons of notes.

"Two months ago," the doctor said, "a writer came to see us. He was researching my great-great-grandfather, Bartholomew Harrington-Smythe."

He turned and pointed to a large painting on the wall. It was of a man with a top hat and a white beard.

"The writer told us that Bartholomew was a criminal. We were shocked, weren't we, dear?" he asked.

"Shocked!" Mrs. Harrington-Smythe replied. "Shocked."

The doctor continued. "He said Bartholomew had killed a young woman in the next village. Terrible. Terrible." He wiped his forehead with his handkerchief.

"Soon after we learned this," his wife said, "I saw the ghosts for the first time."

I scribbled notes as fast as I could. "How often do they come?" I asked.

"The poor woman comes every night," the doctor replied, "screaming and pacing the floor. It's awful. I can't stand it. We'll have to sell the house."

There was a pause as the two old people looked at me.

"Have no fear," I said. "I am here to help."

I stood up and revealed my identity.

I flung off my coat.

I removed my shades.

I ripped off my false mustache.

"I have tricked you," I said. "I am not a reporter at all. I am Damian Drooth, famous kid detective, and I have come to get rid of these terrible ghosts."

The doctor's mouth fell open. "Damian Drooth? Boy genius?" he said. "I read about you in the paper. I'm so grateful that you're here."

"Grateful, grateful," said Mrs. Harrington-Smythe, smiling.

I already had a plan worked out. After Annabelle's grandma got us some orange juice and cake, I explained it all.

"I will come and spend Saturday night in the house," I said.

Harry dug me in the ribs. "Don't forget me," he said. "You promised."

I took another slice of chocolate cake.

"But won't you be terrified?" asked Mrs. Harrington-Smythe.

I shook my head. "A detective only looks at the facts. First, I need to do some research."

We made time to eat a doughnut and then we left, promising we would be back in two days.

Chapter 3

The following day, I called a meeting of my trainee detectives at the playground. Winston, Harry, Todd, and his sister, Lavender (who is only six).

"I don't know much about ghosts," I said. "So I need to find out about them. We'll go down to the library after school and do some serious research. Okay?"

They were all very excited.

That afternoon, we met outside the library. Todd and Lavender brought Curly, who is a very smart dog and part of our Detective School.

"I bet Ms. Travis will be pleased to see us," I said. (Ms. Travis was the librarian. We hadn't seen her for weeks.)

She was behind the desk when we walked in. I thought she looked nervous.

"Damian!" she said. "I see you've brought your friends with you."

"Yes," I replied. "We're doing research."

"Research?" she said, as if she didn't know what it meant.

"Research on ghosts," I said. We headed toward the shelf with books beginning with G.

But Ms. Travis shouted, "Damian! Please go wipe your feet. Now!"

Just to make her happy, we all went back and very carefully wiped the mud off our shoes. But was that enough? No!

"And take your dog outside," she said, pointing to Curly. "They are not allowed in the library."

Todd was shocked. "But it's cold outside," he said. "She could get pneumonia."

"Yeah," said Lavender. "She might die."

I leaned over Ms. Travis's desk and mentioned, ever so quietly, that dogs had rights the same as humans.

"Not in my library they don't," Ms. Travis shrieked.

Then Lavender burst into tears at the very thought of her precious dog being left tied to a drainpipe. "She's going to die," she hollered. The other kids joined the protest.

"It's not right."

"You wouldn't like being left outside."

"Dogs have feelings too, you know."

There was a line forming of people who wanted to check out books. They weren't happy. They were probably dog lovers. Ms. Travis looked worried.

"No worries, Ms. Travis," I said. "Curly is very well-behaved. You do your work and I'll do mine."

We turned and walked toward the non-fiction section, where we carefully tied Curly to the leg of a chair.

There were tons of books on ghosts. We spread them out across two tables.

We spent a long time (at least fifteen minutes) looking through the books. This is what we found out:

Some people don't believe in ghosts.

Ghosts walk through walls.

Ghosts are unhappy because they probably murdered somebody.

Ghosts don't like
Garlic
Crosses
Mirrors
bright Lights
anything that
Smells bad.

The trainee detectives were getting bored.

Lavender and Harry were playing Hide and Seek around the bookshelves. Winston and Todd were kicking a ball of paper across the floor. Even the dog was whining. I don't blame them. It's hard work doing research.

"Okay," I said when I had finished. "Let's go."

We were just walking out through the door when Ms. Travis, who had been very busy reading books and stuff, called out, "Damian!" and waved her hand in the air.

I waved back. "Bye, Ms. Travis."

She waved more frantically. "What about all the books you left on the table?"

"Thanks, Ms. Travis," I said. "They were very helpful."

It always pays to be polite.

Chapter 4

This was my plan for getting rid of the gruesome ghosts:

I would tell Mom I was having a sleepover at Harry's house. Harry would tell his mom he was coming to mine.

It was a great idea.

"That's a great idea," said Harry.

When I told Mom about the sleepover, she seemed really happy.

It turned out she was having some friends over for dinner that night.

"That's a great idea," she said (which is exactly what Harry said).

"Glad you think so, Mom," I replied.

"Well, sometimes you do ruin things when I have people over, Damian."

Some mothers can be so critical.

On Saturday morning, I spent time gathering the things on my list.

1. Garlic. There were two bulbs of garlic on the counter. That wasn't enough, so I took the onions too. Still not enough, so I dug up the leeks in the garden. Leeks are like onions, which are like garlic, so they'd be fine. I planned to make a garlic circle around the house. That would frighten the spooks.

2. Wooden cross. Harry was making a wooden cross. His dad had lots of wood in the garage. He is really good at woodwork.

3. Mirror. Lavender brought a mirror from her bedroom, but it wouldn't work. It was pink and had "My Little Princess" written on the frame in diamonds. There was no way I was taking that. Instead, I went into Mom's bedroom and took the mirror off the wall. It was bad luck that it slipped. But it didn't smash. There was only a crack. Mom would never notice.

By five o'clock, I'd packed my bag and added a few snacks. I believe that ghost watching can make you really hungry.

Mom came with me to the front door. "I want you to be on your best behavior at Harry's house," she said.

She talked about brushing my teeth, remembering my manners, not burping at the table, not picking my nose, and not arguing at bedtime.

Once I'd left our house, I walked to Annabelle's grandparents' house. My team was waiting by the gates.

"Okay," I said, opening my gym bag. "Surround the house with this." I tipped out the garlic, the onions, and the leeks.

"Do you think it'll work?" Harry asked.

"Dunno," I said. "We'll just try everything."

We did our best, but there wasn't enough to go around the house. Instead, we made a big pile in front of the door. That was the next best thing.

Then they went home, leaving Harry and me to do the real work.

Inside the house, there was a fantastic meal waiting for us. Annabelle's grandma had cooked hamburgers, mashed potatoes, and peas, with apple pie and ice cream for dessert. It was delicious.

I was so full that I didn't really feel like ghost hunting. I wanted to just relax and watch TV. But no. A detective never sleeps. I had work to do.

"Where are we going to spend the night?" I asked as Annabelle's grandpa served us chocolates.

"The ghosts appear in our bedroom," he said. "You'll probably want to stay there."

"Oh," said his wife. "You boys are so brave. Won't you be terrified?"

"I'm cool," I said. "I've faced serious criminals before this. A couple of ghosts aren't going to scare me off."

"Me either," said Harry.

"Okay," said Dr. Harrington-Smythe. "I'll take you upstairs."

Chapter 5

The house was just like Dracula's castle — dark and very spooky. As we followed the doctor slowly up the stairs, every step creaked. CREEEAAKKK!

At the top of the stairs was a hallway. It smelled funny and was lit by one single light bulb. The whole house was freezing cold.

The doctor stopped outside a large oak door. "This is our bedroom," he said. "I hope you'll be comfortable."

He opened the door, which creaked very loudly. CREEEAAKKK!

"Candles are by the bed," he said. "Just in case you need them. We've been having a lot of blackouts lately."

You should have seen the bedroom.
It was huge — about twenty times the
size of mine at home. There was one
of those four-poster beds they have in
horror movies with curtains around
them. When the doctor was gone, Harry
jumped onto it and started using it like a
trampoline.

"It's awesome," said Harry. "But I wish
there was a TV in here." He sank onto
the mattress. "Do you have anything to
eat, Damian?"

I was hungry too. It had been at least
half an hour since we finished dinner.
I pulled a bag of tortilla chips from my
gym bag. The chips were in a fancy
bag, but they were just regular chips. I'd
found them in my kitchen with a couple
of tubs of dip.

"Anything else?" Harry asked.

I took out two huge slices of strawberry cake, which I had found in the fridge. They looked really good.

"We should have a midnight feast," said Harry.

But we decided we couldn't wait that long. So we spread the food out on the bed like a picnic and helped ourselves.

Then I realized that I had to go to the bathroom. Bravely, I stepped out into the spooky hallway. I walked down, opening all the doors, but I couldn't find a bathroom.

Then the bulb dangling from the ceiling began to flicker. Flicker, flicker, flicker. Then it went out. Suddenly, I was alone in the dark. What should I do?

With my heart pounding, I put my hands flat on the wall and tried to feel my way back to the bedroom. But then a figure appeared in the dark, glowing a ghostly white. It was moving slowly toward me. Behind it was a smaller shape, misty and almost invisible.

I had never seen a ghost before. Now I was face to face with two of them, I did the only thing I could think of.

I screamed.

I ran back down the hallway, barged into the bedroom, and slammed the door behind me.

Harry was sitting on the edge of the bed, lighting a candle. "The power went out," he said.

"The ghosts turned it off," I yelled. "They're in control. They're in the hallway."

"What are you talking about, Damian?" asked Harry, putting a lit candle on the bedside table.

"Ghosts!" I said. "I saw them. Help me move this dresser in front of the door. We have to keep them out."

Harry's brain might be slow, but he is very strong. Together, we pushed the dresser across the room. We heaved and we shoved until it blocked the door.

Then Harry said, "Ghosts can walk through walls, can't they?"

Harry is not usually right. But that time he was. Nowhere was safe. We were in deadly danger.

Chapter 6

As the head of a famous detective school, I had to set a good example and hide my fear from Harry. Then I heard a noise.

OOOOOOOOOOHHHHHHH!!!!!!

I leapt onto the bed, grabbing the wooden cross, and held it in front of me.

"You don't scare me," I yelled. "I have the tools to finish you off."

This was bold talk. I hoped it would scare the ghosts away.

But the noise came again.

WAAAAAaaaaaaaa!

My stomach began to churn like chocolate in a chocolate factory. How long did we have before the gruesome ghosts appeared in the bedroom?

I must admit, Harry didn't seem bothered. He was pressing his ear against the door. "Listen!" he said. "The ghost is saying 'What?'"

what?

what?

"What?" I said.

"Yes, 'what'."

"What?" I said again.

"Yes, that's what it's saying."

He wasn't making any sense.

"Come here, Damian," he insisted. "Listen again."

Just to make him happy, I put my ear to the door. I was amazed. I could hear real words.

"What's going on?" said the voice.

We pushed the dresser out of the way and opened the door. There was Dr. Harrington-Smythe in a long white bathrobe. His wife was standing next to him in a long white nightie.

Are you surprised I made a mistake? Anyone would have thought they were ghosts.

"We heard you scream," the doctor said. "I thought you were worried when the lights went out."

I shook my head. "The dark doesn't frighten me. I stay cool."

"Well, if you're sure . . ."

"Sure. Don't you worry about us," I said. "In fact, we can't wait to come face to face with the ghosts."

The doctor smiled. I think he felt reassured that we were on the job. Soon they would be saying goodbye to all their problems.

Mrs. Harrington-Smythe, who was carrying a candlestick, said, "We're going to bed now, dears. The electricity should be back on in the morning. Good night."

They turned and headed down the hallway. We shut the door.

"So there weren't any ghosts," said Harry.

"No. You didn't need to be worried," I said.

"I wasn't worried," said Harry.

"What did I tell you?" I said. "It pays to stay calm."

We agreed to take turns to keep watch through the night. Harry climbed into the bed. Soon he was snoring like an old goat.

I sat in an armchair, fully alert, with my notebook in my hand.

But, at exactly ten past eleven, IT HAPPENED.

The doorknob turned. I sat bolt upright and fixed my eyes on the big oak door as it opened very, very slowly. The old hinges creaked. Spooky, spooky, spooky!

But was I scared?

No.

Did I panic?

No.

Did I yell?

No.

This time I was ready.

Chapter 7

First came the noise. *OOOOOOOOOH!*

Then came a blast of cold air as a ghost slowly drifted through the open door and into the room. It was white from head to toe, except for the black top hat. It was just like the man in the painting, beard and all. It was the murdering ancestor of Dr. Harrington-Smythe.

Of course, I wasn't frightened, but I decided to hide under the bed. This was so I could watch what was going on without being seen.

I didn't have long to wait before a second ghost came in. This one was white, too, but much smaller. She wore a gray shawl. She was carrying a bundle, which I guessed was a baby.

I was certain it was the ghost of the woman who had been murdered.

What happened next was horrifying. From my hiding place, I could see the man-ghost turn to the woman-ghost and grab her by the throat, making her scream. It was such a terrible scream that I had to cover my ears.

Aaaaaaaaaggggggggggghhhh!

Then I felt the bed begin to shake. Harry had woken up. At first I thought he was trembling with fear, but no. The bed was shaking because Harry was swinging on the four-poster bed, just like Tarzan. He swung several times before letting go and lunging at the man-ghost.

"Leave her alone, you bully!" he yelled. Then he kicked the man-ghost in the belly.

The ghost yelled, "Aaaaaaaaaagh!" and fell back, staggering toward the door. He dropped his top hat. Then I knew he wasn't a ghost. Under his hat was thick, dark hair. It was all a trick.

But he didn't hang around. He was out of the room in a flash.

"Go after him, Harry," I yelled from under the bed.

Unfortunately, the man-ghost ran down the hallway and climbed out through a window before Harry moved.

"Don't just stand there, Harry!" I yelled. "Stop the other one!"

But the woman-ghost was smart. She flung her shawl over Harry's head, pushed him out of the way, and ran out through the door.

"Too bad," I said, getting out from under the bed. "Try to be faster next time."

Seconds later, there was the sound of breaking glass followed by a scream. The woman-ghost had slipped as she climbed out of the window and she'd fallen onto the greenhouse.

"Let's go, Harry," I said. "Follow me to the garden."

All this noise had woken Annabelle's grandparents. They ran out of the guest bedroom.

As we dashed past, I yelled, "Everything's under control," but they followed behind, as fast as the doctor's creaking knees would allow.

As we ran out the front door, I jumped over the pile of onions, garlic, and leeks.

Harry jumped over them too. But the doctor didn't see them and he tripped over the onions, garlic, and leeks. Then Mrs. Harrington-Smythe tripped over her husband.

We didn't have time to help. We had a crime to solve.

Harry and I hurried across the lawn until we reached the vegetable garden. We were in luck! The woman-ghost was limping between the rows of beans. So I dashed forward and jumped in front of her, holding my wooden stake and garlic.

"I am Damian Drooth," I said, "and I am arresting you for . . ."

"What?" she said. "You're just a kid."

She whacked me with the baby (which wasn't even real). Then she pushed me and Harry into a prickly blackberry bush. It was very painful.

By this time, Annabelle's grandma was back on her feet. She bashed the ghost-woman over the head with a bunch of onions and sent her flying. So that was okay.

One ghost down. One to go.

"The man-ghost must be around somewhere," I whispered to Harry as I tried to remove some nasty thorns from my behind. "There's no way he got away."

"What do we do, Damian?" Harry asked.

"I have a plan," I said.

It was obvious to me that there must be a getaway car somewhere nearby. We walked out to the street and I spotted it. It was a flashy red car parked near the gate. In my experience, this is the kind of car that crooks use.

"Watch and learn," I said to Harry.

I sneaked up to the red car, bent down, and let the air out of the front tires, then the back tires. But before I could finish, I saw the man-ghost come running toward me.

"Hide," I said to Harry. We stepped back into the shadows.

We watched as the man-ghost ran for the car. But he didn't get in the red one. He jumped in an old green one instead.

Was that bad luck or what?

Chapter 8

I have to admit that, for once, our local police were great.

As the man-ghost pulled away from the curb, a police car, with lights flashing and siren blaring, came speeding down the road. It skidded to a halt, blocking the road and stopping him from going anywhere.

I ran over to the police officer as she climbed out.

"Just in time," I said. "I am Damian Drooth, ace detective. I'm sure Inspector Crockitt has mentioned me."

She gave me a funny look. "I am Officer Green," she said. "Did you let the air out of these tires, young man?"

Apparently, the man who lived next door to Annabelle's grandparents was the owner of the red car. He saw me and called the police.

I said, "I have information that will be useful to the Case of the Gruesome Ghosts." I pointed to the man-ghost in the green car. "It was him!"

"He let the air out of the tires?" she asked. Officer Green marched over to the man-ghost. When he tried to escape, she realized he was up to no good.

Anyway, things moved fast after that. A blue car came speeding down the road, followed by a white van.

They both screeched to a halt behind the police car. I recognized them right away.

It was Mom (driving the white van) and Harry's mom and dad (driving the blue car).

"DAMIAN!" Mom shouted. She didn't look very happy. I wondered if her dinner party hadn't been fun.

I tried to tell her what was going on. She wouldn't listen to any of it.

You'd think she would be interested to hear how her son had uncovered the ghost scam.

But she wasn't.

"You lied to me," she said. "I was terrified when I found out you weren't at Harry's house. It was only thanks to Todd and Lavender that I knew where you were."

I made a note to have a serious chat with Todd and his sister. Giving away information about a case was not something that a good detective did.

Mom didn't calm down.

"Not only did you go off without telling me, but you took food that I'd made for my dinner party," she yelled.

Whoops.

Mom was shouting.

Harry's mom and dad were shouting.

The owner of the red car was jumping up and down and yelling about his tires.

The woman-ghost was shrieking at Annabelle's grandpa as he dragged her to the police car.

The ghost-man was crying and Officer Green was arresting him.

Then somebody living nearby called 911 because we were all making so much noise. Three more police cars came and made the road look like a parking lot.

I was relieved to see that Inspector Crockitt was in one of the police cars.

"Damian!" he said, as he stepped out of the car. "Why am I not surprised that you are involved in this?"

I smiled and turned to Officer Green. "See? I told you I was famous." That showed her.

"You'd better come down to the station, Damian," said Inspector Crockitt.

"Cool," I said. "I'm always willing to help the police."

Chapter 9

The case was all over the news. It turned out that Bob Snell, the local real estate agent, and his assistant, Primrose Dobbs, had been

pulling off their crime for weeks. They switched off the electricity at the Harrington-Smythes' house. Then they broke in, dressed as ghosts.

They wanted to scare Annabelle's grandparents into selling their home so they could build smaller houses there and make millions.

"I knew the ghosts weren't real," I explained to Annabelle on Monday.

"Were you scared, Damian?" she asked. She was obviously impressed.

"Nah," I said. "Some people might be really frightened sleeping in that spooky old place. It was no big deal for me."

Harry snorted. "If you weren't scared, why did you hide under the bed?" But I ignored him. He's got a lot to learn.

As usual, nothing I did made my mom happy. She made me do tons of work around the house, like vacuuming and dusting.

"You have to learn to behave responsibly," she said. And she couldn't resist complaining about the garden. "Why did you dig up my leeks?"

I didn't bother trying to explain.

At least Annabelle's grandparents were happy that I'd saved them from a pair of criminals. They invited me and Annabelle to a party. (Harry couldn't come because he failed his math test and had to do extra work.)

While Annabelle ate, I described all the detective tricks I use. I explained my plan for catching her grandparents' ghosts, step by step. Just as I was about to list my ideas about Criminal Types, she suddenly remembered that she had to clean out her guinea pig's cage.

I offered to go with her so that we could keep talking. But she just said, "I don't think so, Damian. Thanks for the advice. You never know, I might even start my own Detective School."

Then she started to giggle.

I'll never understand girls.

About the Author

Barbara Mitchelhill started writing when she was seven years old. She says, "When I was eight or nine, I used to pretend I was a detective, just like Damian. My friend, Liz, and I used to watch people walking down our street and we would write clues in our notebooks. I don't remember catching any criminals!" She has written many books for children. She lives in Shropshire, England, and gets some of her story ideas when she walks her dogs, Jeff and Ella.

About the Illustrator

Tony Ross was born in London in 1938. He has illustrated lots of books, including some by Paula Danziger, Michael Palin, and Roald Dahl. He also writes and illustrates his own books. He has worked as a cartoonist, graphic designer, and art director of an advertising agency. When he was a kid, he wanted to grow up to be a cowboy.

Glossary

criminal (KRIM-uh-nuhl)—someone who commits a crime

disguise (diss-GIZE)—something that hides your identity

gruesome (GROO-sum)—disgusting, terrible

identity (eye-DEN-ti-tee)—who you are

investigation (in-vess-tuh-GAY-shuhn)—finding out as much as you can about something

obvious (OB-vee-uhss)—easy to see or understand

panic (PAN-ik)—struck with a sudden fear

reputation (rep-yuh-TAY-shuhn)—what other people know or think about you

research (REE-surch)—to study or find out about a subject

scam (SKAM)—a trick

trainee (trane-EE)—someone who is learning or being trained

Discussion Questions

1. How did Damian solve the crime? Who was the most helpful person when it came to solving the case?

2. Do you believe in ghosts? Why or why not? Talk about what you think about ghosts.

3. Annabelle is new to Damian's school. What are some ways to make friends if you are in a new place? How can you help students who are new? Talk about it.

Writing Prompts

1. Write a newspaper article describing what happened in this book. Don't forget to include a headline.

2. Pretend to be Annabelle. Write a letter to a friend from your old school talking about how you feel about your new school.

3. What's your favorite ghost story? Write it down!